Translated by Janet Chevrier
Cover illustration by Éric Puybaret
Layout by Bambook

Original French edition:
24 Histoires de Noël pour attendre Jésus

© 2007 by Mame, Paris
© 2011 by Ignatius Press, San Francisco • Magnificat USA LLC, New York
All rights reserved.
ISBN Ignatius Press 978-1-58617-648-8 • ISBN Magnificat 978-1-936260-28-7

Printed by Tien Wah Press, Malaysia
Printed on June 15, 2011
Job Number MGN 11007
Printed in Malaysia in compliance with the Consumer Protection Safety Act, 2008.

24
Christmas Stories
to Welcome
Jesus

Ignatius

MAGNIFICAT

Contents

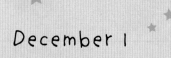

Timothy's Nativity Figurine

That day, Timothy woke up early. A north wind had been blowing all night, and the sky looked brand new. The leaves glistened, and the birds were huddled up together in a ball to protect themselves from the winter chill. It was nice and warm in bed, and Zoe, his stuffed toy mouse with her big furry nose, did not look like she wanted to get up. But this was the big day!

Timothy burst into the kitchen. His hot chocolate was steaming on the table.

"Good morning, sweetheart", said his mom. "I can guess why you're up so early this morning!

"It's the first Sunday in Advent: we're going to start setting up the Nativity scene. And this year, you can choose your own special figurine. That way, it will be as though you're at the manger yourself, waiting for the birth of Jesus!"

Timothy gulped down his breakfast. The big box was ready for him on the living-room table. He lifted the cover—it was like a fluffy cloud inside. He gently dipped his fingers into it: it was so soft. Each figurine was carefully wrapped in cotton and had to be taken out one by one. He felt he was meeting old friends again. And he could choose whichever one he wanted! His mom had prepared the scene with cardboard rocks and stars. Timothy began: the first was a figurine carrying loaves of bread over his shoulder.

"That's the baker", Mom said. "He gets up very early to bake the bread for everyone in the village. But here he is, stopping everything to go see Jesus. He's bringing nice white bread, fresh from the oven, as his gift."

Timothy did not like the idea of getting up very early, so he placed it in the stable, reached back in the box, and found the old shepherd with a black goat. He was carrying a woolen blanket for the Baby Jesus.

"He's a bit of a loner", Mom said. "But even he has come, too, all the way down from the hills, just to see Jesus."

Once again, Timothy hesitated and then put it back down: "I don't want to be an old figurine; and that goat doesn't look very friendly . . . I know that one! She's the woman who sells fish! But Jesus is just a baby. Would he really be happy to get fish as a present?"

"What is important for these figurines, Timothy, is that they offer the best they have to give . . . and, then, Jesus accepts any gift!"

There were a lot of figurines around the manger now. But Timothy still had not found his special one. There was one last figurine in the bottom of the box: it was a tiny little lamb. It had big ears and looked very gentle. "Do you think I could choose this lamb, Mom? I really like him, but he doesn't have any gift!"

"That's not what matters most", Mom reassured him. "The one who waits for Jesus with all his heart until Christmas gives him the most beautiful gift of all!"

The Annunciation to Mary

In her house in Nazareth, Mary is humming. The day of her marriage to Joseph is approaching. Joseph is the carpenter in Nazareth. He is very handsome and very kind. Like Mary's, his faith in God is very strong. Together, what a family they will have!

Ever since she woke up, Mary has had a beautiful prayer on her lips: "I thank you, Lord, with all my heart. I rejoice when I think of all your wonders!

I sing for you, my God!"

Suddenly, a light, gentle wind caresses Mary's face. Where is it coming from? Astonished, she raises her eyes and sees a man, dressed all in white, smiling at her. Mary is so startled, she drops the plate she has been carrying.

But the man looks at her very kindly: "Don't be afraid, Mary, full of grace. My name is Gabriel, and I am an angel of God. He has sent me. I don't want to frighten you; I just want to bring you great news."

Mary does not know what to say. She is stunned. An angel? In her house? What news could he have to announce to her, Mary?

The angel Gabriel continues, smiling at her. "Mary, you are going to have a baby. You will name him Jesus. He will be a king for all men, a king unlike any other. His reign will have no end, and his kingdom will be immense. He will have the power of God."

"A baby?" asks Mary with astonishment. "But how can I have a baby? I'm not even married to Joseph yet!"

The angel Gabriel smiles again. "Nothing is impossible for God, Mary. Listen: your cousin Elizabeth is also expecting a baby, even though she is very old! Everyone thought she would never have a child, and yet, her baby will be born in three months."

Elizabeth, pregnant! What wonderful news for her cousin and her husband, Zechariah!

The angel goes on: "Mary, your baby will come from God. He will be the Son of God, the Savior for whom everyone is waiting."

Mary believes what the angel tells her, and, above all, she wishes for it to be so!

She replies with joy: "I am the servant of the Lord!"

At these words, the angel departs. Overwhelmed by this visit, Mary sits down and, in prayer, thinks over the words that God's messenger has spoken to her. She will keep them deep within her heart, like a hidden treasure, a treasure of great joy.

An Unexpected Early Christmas Gift

Ding, dong!

As soon as Mathilda and Gabriel heard the doorbell, they ran to the stairs.

"I'll go open the door", Gabriel said to his big sister.

"No, I'll go; it's my godmother who's coming for lunch!" Mathilda got to the door first and opened it in delight.

Her godmother had arrived, carrying a big package in her arms! Mom and Dad came to welcome her. Mom laughed and scolded the godmother a little: "A gift? Before Christmas? You spoil your goddaughter too much!"

Mathilda's godmother handed her the package and explained as she took off her coat, "It's not a Christmas present. It's an Advent present, and it's for the whole family."

Mathilda and Gabriel stared wide-eyed.

An Advent present? Whatever could that be? They already had an Advent calendar, with lots of little windows to be opened day by day. So it could not be that.

"What's an Advent present?" asked Mathilda.

Her godmother hugged her as she replied, "It's a gift to help you prepare for Christmas and to give a festive air to the house in the meantime. Go on, open it!"

Mathilda tore open the wrapping paper and found a beautiful wreath of pine branches with a pretty red satin ribbon. In the center were four more little packages of different sizes.

Dad and Mom smiled: "We've already guessed what it is! What a very good idea! Thank you!"

Curious, Mathilda and Gabriel opened the packages. They found four white candles: one very big, one not quite so big, one medium-sized, and one very little.

Mathilda's godmother placed them in the candleholders hidden within the wreath. "There, that's your Advent wreath! Do you know how to use it?" she asked.

"Everyone lights his own candle", said Gabriel. "Dad, the biggest; Mom, the next biggest; Tilly, the middle one; and I light the smallest."

Godmother laughed, "That's a nice idea, but the four candles don't represent the four members of the family. They represent the four weeks of Advent. Do you know what Advent is?"

"It's the time before Christmas", said Mathilda with a grown-up air, "when we await the birth of Jesus."

"And gifts and candy", added Gabriel eagerly.

"Yes, that's right", said Godmother. "Today is the first Sunday of Advent. So we light the first candle, the biggest. Next Sunday, we light the second, and so on. It's a way of saying that Jesus is the light that lights up our life."

Dad laid the wreath on the living-room table and lit the first candle.

"Why aren't the candles all the same size?" asked Mathilda.

"It's because the first one will burn longer than the last", explained Godmother. "That way, on Christmas Eve, they'll all be the same size! It will be prettier like that, won't it? "

The First Living Nativity Scene

The villagers of Greccio, in Italy, have passed down over the centuries this memory of a beautiful Christmas . . .

Francis of Assisi and his friends had chosen to live near the village in a grotto—a kind of cave—in order to live humble lives, just as they had promised each other. Off on their own, the four young companions found the solitude in which to pray. One fine morning, shortly before Christmas, Francis decided they should share the holiday with others.

"I'd like us to have a Christmas celebration here", he announced to the other brothers.

"In the grotto?" asked Brother Rufus with astonishment.

"Wasn't Jesus born in poverty?" Francis replied mischievously. "Didn't the stable in Bethlehem look very much like our grotto?"

"What a good idea!" Brother Leo applauded.

"Then, let's get to work!" cried Francis, as he set off for the village.

A few hours later, mooing could be heard in the mountains. It was Brother Leo, trying to get a cow to climb all the way up to the grotto—not an easy job!

Behind him, Brother Angelo and Brother Rufus followed with a donkey carrying a manger loaned by one of the villagers. In the meantime, Francis was in charge of finding the cast for the Nativity scene: a young girl to play the role of Mary, an adult man to be Joseph, one or two shepherds, and—of course, a baby!

By evening, everything was ready. Young Mary arrived first. She was very moved. Then came the shepherds, each one carrying a lamb over his shoulders. Saint Joseph arrived a little late.

In fact, he was just so shy, he was afraid he would not be up to the role. Finally, a woman laid her baby in the manger. She had placed her baby's arms to his sides and wrapped him up nice and tight so he would not catch cold. The Mass could finally begin . . .

It is said that this first living Nativity scene deeply touched the hearts of the villagers who attended this very special Mass. One particular event left a deep impression on everyone there that night: when, in the distance, the village church bells chimed the twelve strokes of midnight, the baby woke up. He opened his eyes, and he smiled. It was a true Christmas miracle!

If Paul Had Never Existed...

Paul trudged slowly home from school with his head down. Muddy snow covered the sidewalk. Pelting rain crashed down in the headlights of the traffic. This December evening was as sad as Paul's heart. Today, everything had gone wrong! In the morning, he got angry with his mother. Then he got an F in a math test. Finally, he quarreled with Oliver, his best friend!

"There are some days when . . ."

"When what?"

Paul had been talking out loud without realizing it. Someone behind him had heard! Paul turned around and looked carefully at the stranger. Reassured by his curiously bright face, Paul continued, ". . . When I wish I weren't alive. Besides, no one would miss me."

"You think so?" the stranger asked with a smile. "I'd like you to play a little game with me. Imagine you had never existed . . ."

Paul arrived home and stood in the doorway, astonished: Where were the Christmas decorations? What had happened to the Christmas tree? Paul glanced into the living room and saw his mom with Mrs. Morel, Oliver's mother. His mother's beautiful face was worn out with grief, and she suddenly looked very old . . .

"My dear friend," said Mrs. Morel, "you should set out a Nativity scene. The Christmas manger brings such joy to a house!"

"Joy for whom?" sighed Paul's mother. "I couldn't have children. With or without a Nativity scene, my house will never know happiness . . . But let's talk about you; how is your son Oliver?"

Mrs. Morel answered in a worried voice, "He doesn't have any friends, and that makes him so sad! I'm very worried about him."

Paul stared wide-eyed, trying to understand . . . He turned toward the stranger who had been following him, but the mysterious man was looking at an old lady speaking to a policeman in the street. She seemed very upset . . .

"What's happening?" Paul asked the stranger.

"This woman lost her handbag. There was money in it and, more importantly, many precious mementos . . ."

"That's not true!" Paul protested. "I remember that lady. Yesterday, I found her handbag on the bus, and I returned it to her."

"You? You don't exist . . . But, it's true, if you didn't exist, someone would have to invent you!"

And before Paul's astonished eyes, the stranger let out a laugh as light as the peal of church bells. "Farewell, little Paul," he said, "and never forget that your life is a treasure."

And with that he vanished. When Paul went inside, he found the familiar Nativity scene beneath the decorated Christmas tree. His mother came to greet him. Her face was once again young and carefree!

"I'm sorry I was in such a bad mood this morning", mumbled Paul.

"It's nothing, sweetheart. It's already forgotten! Did you have a good day?"

"Not so bad!" answered Paul with a mysterious gleam in his eye. "I think I saw an angel . . ."

The Night of Saint Nicholas

"Go on, girls, get to bed! It's time to go to sleep!"

"Oh, no, Daddy!" Lucy and Florence protested. "We want to stay up a little with Grandma tonight. She's only just got here!"

Grandma smiled and took the little girls into her arms. "That's kind, my sweethearts. But Daddy and Mommy are right. And," Grandma added mysteriously, "if you don't get under the covers right away, Saint Nicholas won't be able to visit. That would be a shame!"

Daddy and Mommy agreed, with a twinkle in their eyes.

"Who's Saint Nicholas?" asked Lucy.

"He's a great saint, sweethearts. A long time ago, he saved the lives of three little children held prisoner by a nasty butcher. Where I come from, in Belgium, he's the one who brings children presents. But, mind you, not just any day—on his feast day, December 6."

Florence clapped her hands with joy, "Hurray! December 6, that's tomorrow!"

Lucy, though, was a little doubtful. "Yes, but if you don't live in Belgium, does he still come?"

Grandma laughed, "Yes, I think so. I spoke to him about you. But, in any case, he'll come only on one condition."

"What is it, what is it?" cried Lucy and Florence with great excitement.

"Well, Saint Nicholas is the friend of well-behaved children . . . who go to bed without making a fuss, for example. Are you well-behaved, my dears?"

"Yes, yes, we're good!"

With that, Lucy and Florence ran right off to their bedroom and quickly jumped into bed. Grandma came to see them and placed a little tray on the windowsill.

"You left in such a hurry, I didn't have time to tell you about his donkey!"

The little girls perked up their ears to listen.

"To carry his presents, Saint Nicholas has a very helpful donkey. He covers miles, the poor thing! And that makes him hungry, very hungry! That's why kind little children prepare a nice carrot for him!"

And Grandma showed them the big carrot on the tray.

Lucy asked, "And the glass of milk, is that for Saint Nicholas?"

"That's right, sweetheart. He often gets a little thirsty during his rounds. Now, everything is ready. Quick, close your eyes: Saint Nicholas brings presents to children only while they sleep! And don't try to pretend; you can't fool Saint Nicholas! Good night!" Grandma softly shut the door.

Lucy and Florence opened their eyes early the next morning, wondering if Saint Nicholas had come to visit.

They quickly looked at the little tray. The carrot was gone, and the glass was empty! But, best of all, next to the glass, someone had left two little golden packages . . .

The Meeting of the Wise Men

The wise man Gaspar is sitting on the edge of a well. He looks at the reflection of a big star dancing on the surface of the water. Now that night has fallen, the star glows with extraordinary brightness. Among all the stars, it is the only one mirrored in the dark water of the well . . .

Suddenly, the reflection vanishes. Raising his eyes, Gaspar sees that the star has moved in the sky.

Just as he does every evening, he wakes up his camel: "Come on, Tabriz, let's get going. The star is calling us to continue our journey!"

Another camel approaches the well, led by an African.

The reflection of the star shines in the stranger's eyes. "Peace be with you, my fellow voyager!" the African greets Gaspar. "My name is Balthazar. I've come all the way from the south of the world following this star. According to my studies in astronomy, it heralds the birth of a great king . . ."

"Then we're going to the same place", replies Gaspar. "I left my country far away in the east to see this royal child. Could we continue our journey together, then?"

"Of course!" says Balthazar.

It is then that a third man arrives at the well. His camel is laden with a chest of gold glinting in the light of the big star.

"Peace be with you! My name is Melchior. I've come from a faraway land, guided by this star."

"So it shines everywhere", says Gaspar with wonder. "It announces its good news to all the world. The king to be born will truly be great!"

All three men gaze up toward the twinkling star and set out again on their journey. "Have you prepared gifts for the Infant King?" Gaspar asks his companions.

"Yes," says Melchior, "I have in this box nuggets of gold, because gold is the most precious metal there is."

"And I", says Balthazar, "am bringing him incense."

"But incense is what you give to God!" says Melchior with surprise.

"I thought it a gift worthy of this great king", answers Balthazar. " . . . And you, Gaspar, my friend, what gift have you brought?"

"Myrrh", answers Gaspar.

"How unfortunate!" exclaims Balthazar. "Don't you know in your country that this precious resin is used to perfume the bodies of the dead? What a strange gift for a newborn!"

"Yes," says Gaspar, nodding his head, "but, one day, who knows? This great king will die, and I won't be there any more to honor him. So . . ."

But Gaspar says no more. The wise men continue their journey in silence beneath the star, turning over in their hearts mixed thoughts of joy and sadness.

28

The Christmas Truce

In Finland, near the town of Turku, Duke John was doing the rounds of his troops just as he did every day. He looked with pity at the tired men. All of them had been drafted to defend Turku against jealous neighbors who longed to conquer their town.

"Soon it will be Christmas, and we would all like to spend the holiday with our families", he thought sadly. "If only we weren't at war . . . If only the fighting could stop just for a little while . . ."

Duke John suddenly pulled on his horse's reins and came to an abrupt halt. He had just had an idea! Without losing a moment, he set off at a gallop toward the enemy lines.

When he arrived before the enemy camp, he stopped his horse and rose in his stirrups. "Tomorrow, if God be willing, shall be a day of grace in honor of the birth of our Lord and Redeemer", he proclaimed in a powerful voice.

"And so we declare a Christmas truce and invite you to celebrate this holy day with the reverence it deserves." The words of the duke of Turku met with a long silence. But soon, shouts of joy went up everywhere, from both camps. "It's a truce!" yelled the soldiers, as they ran toward each other. In a few moments, the battlefield was transformed. Yesterday's enemies greeted one another, shook hands, and embraced.

The men rapidly gathered to form one and the same joyful troop and set off together down the road to the town.

When the women and children of Turku caught sight of the approach of this strange procession, they were frightened and quickly barricaded themselves in their houses.

"Open up! We've come to celebrate Christmas!" shouted Duke John's men in the streets.

"And we have guests!"

Then, one by one, doors opened to welcome the soldiers. The men were reunited with their families, and they all invited their neighbors in with a smile. Joyfulness spread throughout every street. Delicious aromas came from every house. At Midnight Mass, the old enemies raised their voices like brothers in songs of praise for the birth of the Savior.

Ever since then, the mayor of Turku proclaims a Christmas truce each year. For two whole days, all people forget their quarrels in order to prepare for the celebration of the birth of Jesus in peace.

The Visitation

When the angel comes to tell Mary she is to become the mother of the Messiah, he brings her other great news as well.

"Mary!" he tells her, "Your cousin Elizabeth is also with child!" Elizabeth is indeed expecting a baby, who will be named John—she who is already almost an old lady and has thought she would never have the joy of bearing a child. But God truly works wonders! With him, nothing is impossible . . .

Mary hurries to prepare a bag and leaves to go to Elizabeth.

She is eager to share all her secrets with her cousin, whom she loves like a sister.

She cannot wait to congratulate her and to help her prepare for the birth of her baby!

Mary is almost there. She can make out the house of Elizabeth and Zechariah in the distance.

She goes in and hugs her cousin. At that moment, Elizabeth's baby leaps with joy within her womb.

She is filled with the Holy Spirit and the love of God. Something extraordinary has just happened.

She exclaims, "Mary, God chose you from among all women to bear in your womb the Son of God, who is coming to live among us. It is a great honor for me to receive your visit. God had promised to send us someone who would bring joy to all mankind. Well, he has kept his promise.

"The child you are carrying is the one for whom we have been waiting. Blessed are you, Mary. You said Yes to the angel who came to announce this news. You believed in what God had promised."

Mary smiles. She feels a beautiful prayer rise within her. Her heart overflows with thanks, and she finds herself singing: "Thank you, my God, for this baby who is to be born. I am so joyful to have been chosen by you to bear the Savior of the world! Because I'm just a humble girl . . . Truly, my God, you have done wonders for me. Your goodness has been shown to all men. You take care of those who trust in you; you protect the poor and the hungry. You are faithful; you never forget your promises."

God's Surprise

Every night in the fields around Bethlehem, shepherds cloaked in big brown capes keep watch over their flocks until dawn. In the middle of this freezing night, everyone is sleeping but them! A little shepherd looks up at the sky. There is a crescent moon . . .

Suddenly, he points toward the sky: "Look! A new star has just been born; there, right above us. It's more beautiful and brighter than any of the others!"

The old shepherd, who speaks only on special occasions, remains silent for a moment and then murmurs: "You're right . . . That's the first time I've ever seen that star. I think something extraordinary must be happening . . . Joy is about to come to us!"

There is a festive breeze in the air. The little shepherd is so excited, he does a little dance and plays on his flute. "Go get the tambourines!" he yells. "We'll get you all dancing . . ." Everyone wants to speak at the same time.

But one shepherd pipes up, "Do you think it is God who is preparing a surprise for us?"

At that, everyone falls silent. No one knows what to say.

But the old shepherd answers, "If it is God who is preparing a surprise for us, if he cares about us, well . . . we have nothing more to fear. We can be as trusting as this little lamb who lets me cradle him in my arms. We will want for nothing . . ."

Waving his arms all about, the little shepherd exclaims, "Perhaps we'll have nice weather all year! No more cold or snow! We will eat sweets from spring to New Year!"

The old shepherd continues, "I haven't laughed for years; but today, even I feel like dancing.

"I know this mysterious joy comes from God. The surprise he's preparing for us will change our lives! Perhaps the Savior for whom we have been waiting is coming to us! Even if we are always by ourselves in the fields with our flocks . . . we know that God has not forgotten us!"

The little shepherd is in a great hurry. "Enough talking! We must find this surprise from God!"

He cannot stand still a moment longer, but he does not really know where to go.

"Let's follow the star", the old shepherd suggests. "Come on! Let's go, hurry up, we're going to be late!"

The sheepdogs lead the way. The old shepherd takes hold of his walking-stick in one hand and the little shepherd's arm with the other. The flock goes forward with bleating and bells jangling. They all walk in the night, climbing hills, skipping over little streams, singing, dancing, laughing . . . Their hearts rejoice already at the thought that they might be going to see their Savior.

The Fourth Wise King

Hannibal has seen the star rising, too. Like Melchior, Gaspar, and Balthazar, he knows right away that something important is happening. Looking through his books, he discovers that this star heralds the birth of the Savior. So Hannibal takes the three most beautiful pearls from his treasure to offer them to the Child and sets off down the road. Hannibal has been walking a long time with his nose in the air, trying not to lose sight of the star, when he trips over something.

A man is lying in the road.

"What are you doing here?" he asks, taking pity on the man.

"I'm waiting to die", the man answers in a weak voice. "I'm sick and I have no money to pay to be nursed."

Hannibal does not hesitate a second. He helps the sick man up and leads him to the nearest town. There, he entrusts him to an old lady and gives her his first pearl.

"With this pearl you will be able to buy whatever this man needs", he says before leaving.

Hannibal is setting off again along the road, with his nose in the air, when he hears cries. A man is striking a woman violently.

"What has she done?" he asks with compassion.

"She's a slave, a good-for-nothing!" the man answers nastily. "She doesn't do her work properly."

Without hesitation, Hannibal takes another pearl from his money bag.

"Take it", he says, handing it to the man. "I'll buy this woman's freedom from you. Let her go."

The man grabs the pearl and lets go of the young woman.

"Thank you", she murmurs to Hannibal before fleeing.

The wise king continues on his journey, with his nose in the air.

He has almost reached Bethlehem when a widow runs up to him in tears.

"What's wrong, madam?" he asks her gently.

"The soldiers have taken my son away!" she sobs. "He stole some flour so I could have something to eat! He's all I have left in the world!"

This time, too, Hannibal does not hesitate a second. He follows the widow to the prison. There, he gives his last pearl to the soldiers, who set their prisoner free. The mother is reunited with her son. As for Hannibal, he hurries off faster than ever, because he is already late.

When Hannibal arrives at the manger, the first three wise kings have already offered their gifts to the newborn and have left. Arriving empty-handed, all he has to offer are his apologies. And yet, the Baby Jesus welcomes him with a big smile and outstretched arms. Is not the visit of such a generous wise man the most beautiful gift of all?

A Nurse Like No Other

"Christmas is the most beautiful day of the year, except when you spend it in the hospital", little Marion thought sadly, as she fidgeted in her bed. For many months now, she had been receiving treatment for a serious illness. Yesterday, the doctor had operated on her. Now, on the night before Christmas, while other children were hanging up their stockings, Marion was brooding gloomily . . .

As her stitches hurt, she pressed the buzzer on her bed to call a nurse. A moment later, the door of her room opened. A young nurse came to the bed, leaned over Marion, and gave her a kiss on the forehead.

The little girl was very surprised. "That's the first time a nurse ever gave me a kiss! Usually, they just give me a shot! Are you new? I've never seen you before . . ."

"What's wrong?" asked the nurse by way of an answer.

"I hurt . . . It's not fair to spend Christmas in the hospital! I'm afraid I'll never get better", sighed Marion.

The nurse took the little girl into her arms and began speaking to her in a soothing voice. And her words went right to Marion's heart like so many little drops of courage . . .

"In one hour, the scouts will come to sing and play with the sick children. You'll have a wonderful afternoon . . ."

MARION

"Then your parents will arrive. You'll go together to Christmas Mass in the hospital chapel. They'll stay to keep you company late into the night. And you'll soon get better and will get back to normal life."

"How do you know all that?" Marion asked with astonishment.

"I'm never wrong. And I never lie to children."

Marion looked carefully at this strange nurse. She had sparkling eyes and a smile as bright as a sunbeam. Just looking at her gave Marion back her appetite for life!

"Why is your smock such a bright green?" asked the little girl, who was good at noticing unusual details. "It almost looks like the color of trees in springtime!"

"You're getting back your curiosity, then; that's a good sign!" smiled the nurse. "My smock is like this because joyful green is my color."

"Oh, right . . ." said Marion, not really understanding this funny kind of answer. "And, what's your name?"

"Hope", the nurse simply replied.

"That's a pretty name", exclaimed Marion, with a dreamy look in her eye. The nurse gave the little girl another hug.

"I'm going to visit the other patients now. They all need me today! But I'll stay very close to you. If you start feeling sad again, all you need to do is call me."

Saint Lucy's Day

It was still pitch black when Olga woke up on this feast-day morning. In Sweden, on December 13, every family celebrates Saint Lucy's Day. According to tradition, Olga put on a long white dress, tied a beautiful red silk sash around her waist, and proudly placed a crown with five white candles on her head. Her brothers and sisters put on costumes, too. The girls wore white dresses and silver crowns; the boys wore big star-spangled hats. The children prepared breakfast in the kitchen as a surprise for their parents. Everyone was busy.

The boys placed two steaming mugs of coffee on a large tray. The girls took out of the cupboard the thousand and one delicacies they had prepared the night before: saffron rolls, little cookies in the shape of stars, hearts, and gingerbread men.

When everything was ready, Theodore, the oldest of the children, lit the candles of Olga's crown. The children turned off all the lights. Olga led the way through the shadows, all lit up. Awakened by shouts of joy, their parents opened their eyes to find their five delighted children around their bed. Everyone exchanged kisses and warm greetings and shared a wonderful breakfast. Suddenly, Olga had an idea: "Let's go for a walk in the town! With my crown, I'll light your way!"

Soon, the parents and the children were outside, all wrapped up. The sun had not risen yet, because the night of the feast of Saint Lucy is the longest night of winter. And yet, there were lights all over the town: little lamps, lights, and candles were glowing in the windows.

The children skipped and sang. They joined hands as Olga led them dancing through the streets, her magical crown swaying in the frosty air . . .

And so Olga chased the darkness away!

The Canticle of Giacomo

The old musician Giacomo was in a very grumpy mood. In a few days, it would be Christmas. And he did not like Christmas.

"I don't believe in this story: a God who's born in a stable? . . . What nonsense!" he mumbled into his beard. Giacomo was still grumbling when someone knocked on his door.

"What is it?" he asked gruffly, as he opened the door.

"Excuse me," replied a young man, "I didn't mean to disturb you!" Giacomo's voice softened as he asked his visitor in.

"I'm sorry," he said, "I'm a crotchety old man. What can I do for you?"

"I'm the new priest in the parish", the young man explained. "I've come to commission a new Christmas canticle from you!"

You could have knocked Giacomo down with a feather! "A Christmas canticle!? Well, that's the best I've ever heard", he said under his breath. "But, why not? After all, I need the work at the moment."

"I'll do it!" he finally agreed.

"I'm delighted", responded the priest with a smile. "I'll come to get it before Midnight Mass."

Giacomo set to work straightaway. The old man scratched his head as he sat in front of the blank page. How difficult to write a Christmas canticle when you do not believe in Jesus! How hard to sing the joy of Christmas when you do not like this holiday!

Giacomo scribbled, crossed things out, and discarded dozens of pages. Soon, exhausted, he fell asleep at his desk and began to dream. He dreamed that an angel came in through the window and whispered in his ear.

The angel told him the story of Christmas night, when a baby had been born to save the world and to love all mankind. The angel whispered to him that this child had come for Giacomo, too . . .

He revealed to him the gentleness of this God who had arrived so meekly, in a stable, so as not to impose himself on men. In his sleep, Giacomo smiled. When he woke up in the middle of the night, the old musician took a clean sheet of paper. And he began to write and write . . .

"Come, let us adore him, this newborn child!
He, the greatest, so little, so mild,
Come, let us adore him! Come, tell the world:
Today he is born to save us all . . ."

Giacomo could not stop writing; his heart was overflowing with gratitude for this God he had just discovered. So, he composed music all through the night, never stopping until dawn.

That year, Christmas Midnight Mass was more beautiful than ever before. And, as the parishioners sang his canticle, old Giacomo, seated at the back of the church, prayed for the first time in his life.

A Generous Pirate

"What are you doing, Martin?" Dad asked with surprise.

Martin was sitting in his room in the middle of an incredible mess. All around him, he had unpacked boxes of old toys that had been stored at the back of his closet . . .

"The school is organizing a Christmas collection", the little boy explained. "All the students can bring gifts. They'll be given to kids less fortunate than we are, to share the joy of Christmas with them."

"That's an excellent idea", Dad said. "And what are you going to donate?"

"Maybe my train set; I don't play with it anymore."

Dad smiled.

"You know, Martin, true giving means offering something for which you really care. You could share half of something that means a lot to you. Your marble collection, for instance . . . But I don't want to interfere;

it's none of my business. I'll let you make your choice in peace." Left alone, Martin thought this over. He knew his dad was right. "Sharing is beautiful . . . but difficult!" he said, thinking out loud.

Martin opened the closet. There on a hanger was his favorite costume, a magnificent pirate outfit. Without hesitation, the little boy unhooked the sword and the plumed hat and kept the boots and the black bandanna for himself. That just left the pirate captain's bright red cape!

He stroked it with his fingers. But how could he share it? Martin thought a moment and could find only one solution. He went to find a pair of scissors . . .

Snip, snip! The scissors cut into the beautiful red velvet. Martin set to it with all his heart: he had to cut the fabric nice and straight, right down the middle . . . There! The cape was cut in two!

It was then that Mom came into the room.

"What have you done, Martin?" she asked with dismay. "Why have you ruined the beautiful costume I gave you?"

Unhappy to have upset his mother, Martin sheepishly explained.

What a surprise! A big smile suddenly lit up his mom's face . . .

"It's funny, Martin. Your patron saint did exactly the same thing. He was a soldier in the Roman Empire. One freezing night, that Martin came across a beggar on the road dying from the cold. He stopped his horse, unsheathed his sword, and . . . he cut the cape of his uniform in two and gave half to the beggar!"

Astonished, Martin looked at the two capes in his hand.

Mom went on, "These capes still look very dashing! Your gift will make the little boy who receives it very happy. I'm proud of you, Martin."

"Me, too", added Dad, who had silently come in and was looking at the scene with an amused and happy smile.

The Littlest of the Empire

This year, the roads of Judea are filled with travelers.

Caesar Augustus, the emperor of Rome, has ordered a census: he has decided to count all the people in his vast empire. Each of his subjects has to go to his hometown to have his name entered on the lists.

Judea is a faraway province of the Roman Empire. In obedience to the emperor, all of its inhabitants set off to the place where they were born . . .

On the road to Bethlehem, the wind blows up a dust storm. The travelers move closer together and talk to each other to keep up their spirits.

Seated on a donkey, a young woman seems lost in thought.

She smiles to herself, or rather to the baby she is expecting, for she is stroking her round belly with her hand . . .

"Your pregnancy seems far advanced!" remarks a woman walking beside her, holding a little boy by the hand. "Where have you come from? Where do you have to go?"

"We've come from Nazareth, and we're going to Bethlehem", answers the young woman.

"You'll be there soon. But I hope you won't give birth there! This morning, I came across a man returning from Bethlehem. According to him, all the inns in town are full. They're turning people away!"

"May God's will be done", the young woman answers with serenity.

"Don't worry, I'll find us shelter somehow, Mary!" her husband promises in a firm voice. "As sure as my name is Joseph, you won't give birth out in the cold."

The little boy holding his mother's hand does not miss a word of the conversation. He looks at Mary, so delicate yet so confident. He looks carefully at Joseph, so solid and determined.

Suddenly, he asks in a clear voice, "If your baby is born in Bethlehem, will he be enrolled in the census, too?"

Surprised and amused, Joseph looks down at the child. "That's a good question, little one. I should think so! Caesar wants to count all the inhabitants of his empire: this baby, when he arrives, will be part of it . . ."

Mary's smile grows bigger. She thinks of the emperor of Rome bent over the enormous list of the inhabitants of his empire. She imagines Caesar's satisfaction when he discovers he is reigning over so many subjects. And if he has the patience to read the list right to the end, he will find the name of little Jesus, born in Bethlehem in the last days of the census . . . How could he guess that the birth of this littlest inhabitant of his empire will be the greatest news ever told?

The Old Gray Wolf and the White Sheep

From the dawn of time, wolves have been devouring gentle little sheep. Sometimes, to get their revenge, sheep set traps for the wolves. Very often, the poor things would lose the tips of their tails in them!

It was the day before Christmas. On this lovely, snowy morning, a young sheep took advantage of an open gate to escape the sheepfold and explore the countryside.

The unfortunate thing! Did he not know, then, that an old gray wolf was prowling the forest? Famished after two days without food, the wolf was looking for something to sink his teeth into.

The little white sheep, blissfully unaware, thought of nothing but playing, leaping, and frolicking in the fresh snow. But soon, he had to admit it: he did not recognize anything around him anymore. He was well and truly lost. As he wondered how he could ever find his way back to the sheepfold, he noticed in the snow two black ears, all furry and pointed. Curious, he took a step forward and made out big, long, white teeth, as sharp as the mountain peaks. It was the wolf!

He did not cry "Wolf!" as sheep usually do in stories; he stood stock-still, staring at the enemy. The wolf's mouth was already watering. He licked his lips. He purred with pleasure. The little sheep, a bit frightened by these faces the wolf was making, took a step back toward the river behind him. The wolf, thinking he was trying to escape, set off like mad without looking where he was going and . . . splash! He fell into the river.

"Help! Help!" cried the wolf. "I'm going to drown; I can't swim!" The little sheep hesitated a moment, but, without knowing why, he stretched out a paw to him. "Come on, I'll get you out of there!" Once back on the riverbank, the wolf shivered with cold and fright. Full of generosity, the little sheep suggested, "Let me warm you up. My fleece is soft and warm!" The old wolf was far too proud to let a sheep snuggle up to him! He recovered his deep, grumbling voice, "Why are you still sitting here next to me?

"You really just don't understand anything! Don't you know that wolves devour sheep? If I wanted to, I could eat you up in one bite . . ."

"Perhaps," the sheep answered proudly, "but I'm not just any sheep! I saved your life! And you're not an ungrateful wolf; you surely wouldn't still want to devour me now, would you?"

The old wolf was suddenly tongue-tied. He looked the sheep right in the eye. "Thank you!" he said. "I've never known of another sheep as brave as you. From now on, let's be friends."

That evening was Christmas Eve. The old gray wolf escorted the little white sheep back to his sheepfold. Dancing in the sky to the rhythm of the church bells, thousands of stars lit the way for the two good friends.

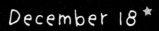

Christmas in the Museum

Jackie was the night guard at the museum. Since her husband died, she preferred living at night so that she did not have to see everyone else laughing and having fun all around her. Normally, the job of a museum guard was quiet and uneventful. Between her rounds, Jackie passed the time reading books about painting and carefully studying the artwork on exhibit. This evening, for the first time, Jackie heard voices in one of the museum rooms. Yet, during her last rounds, she was sure she had not seen anyone . . .

Her heart pounding, the guard grabbed her flashlight and went toward the big room from which she thought the voices were coming. She approached cautiously and listened. There was no doubt about it: there were people behind the door! It almost sounded as if someone were playing music. She carefully pushed the door open and stuck her head around it. But it was no use; there was nothing to see. The room was empty! No one was there!

She entered the room to make sure nothing was missing. The paintings were all there, hanging straight in their places.

But . . . how strange! There was something about the paintings. Jackie thought they did not look quite the same! The musicians, the noblemen, the royal ladies, all of the people in the paintings seemed to have changed: the women looked more beautiful than usual; the men looked fresh-shaven; the musicians appeared to have polished their instruments. Everything in the room was brighter, merrier. Most of all, Jackie had the impression that all the people in the portraits were facing toward the center of the room where there was a little painting of Mary, Joseph, and the Christ Child.

Then Jackie realized: it was almost Christmas!

In the past, like the noble ladies in these paintings, she too would get dressed up for the occasion. She remembered the joyful moments spent with her family, and she thought of Midnight Mass, where she used to like singing. For the first time in a long while, Jackie felt a wave of sweetness fill her heart. The people in the portraits had reminded her of the joy of Christmas. Thanks to them, she once again felt like celebrating the birth of Jesus!

Upon hearing this story, many of you will think Jackie was just dreaming that evening. Who knows?

But one thing is sure: she asked not to have to guard the museum on Christmas night. And she put on her most beautiful dress to go to Midnight Mass.

The Old Ox of Bethlehem

"Go on, move over, lazy!"

At these words, the old ox, who has been dozing, gives a start. He understands right away what is happening. His master has just bought a young, very strong, very sturdy ox. Without batting an eyelid, the old animal just moves over and, as soon as his master has left, tries to get back to sleep.

But the young ox is a rather talkative sort. "Excuse me, sir. I didn't want to take your place. I hope you're not too uncomfortable . . ."

"Don't worry about it, little fellow. I've seen it all before!"

And he rolls back over with a great yawn.

Timidly, the young ox goes on, "Oh, really, have there been many oxen before me? Were they strong? Is the work hard?"

The old animal turns over with a sigh. "No, you're the first in years. What I meant was that it's not the first time I've had to move over like that, in the middle of the night. And then, above all, after what I've seen, nothing surprises me any more, I can tell you!"

Intrigued, the young ox asks, "And what exactly have you seen?"

The old ox sits up proudly.

"Well, it was like this. It was a beautiful winter night, and bitter cold, little fellow! To keep warm, I huddled together with my pal the donkey—he died last year. That's when our master came into the stable, shoved us over, and brought in . . ." The storyteller stops for effect. "He brought in a man and his wife, who was expecting a baby. There were such crowds in the village, there wasn't one single room left, so my master put them up as a favor, and, in the night, the baby was born. Such a cute little boy! The donkey and I, we were afraid he'd catch cold. So, while his parents slept, we breathed on him to keep him cozy and warm."

"Oh, really, that's nice . . ."

The young ox does not seem to find the story very remarkable.

The old ox goes on, "Wait!
It's what happened next that was incredible:
shepherds arrived from all over the countryside, and
then some very rich people, with lots of presents."

"Presents? For a baby born in the hay?"

"Exactly. Everyone seemed to take this baby for a king. Even
better: everyone said this child was the Savior for whom men had
been waiting, that he was at last going to bring joy to the world!
So, little fellow, ever since that day, I've understood a lot of
things. To be the strongest, to have the best place, that makes
no difference. But the birth of that Child, now that was
something truly important."

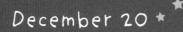
A Christmas Dinner without Borders

In the night, the German customs officer guarding the border had just noticed something suspicious. On the other side of the border, the French customs officer was sending him signals with his lantern! The German slowly worked out the Morse code: "'d–i–n–n–e–r– t–i–m–e'. Whatever did that mean, 'dinnertime'?" In those days, more than a century ago, Germany and France did not get along very well . . .

HALT
GRENZE

Taking his lantern, the German went toward the barrier that marked the border. The French customs officer welcomed him with a big smile.

"Good evening, neighbor! It's almost Christmas. So, this evening, I would like to invite you to share a holiday meal. Christmas is a good occasion to forget the border that separates us, don't you think?" A smile lit the face of the German customs officer. They both went back to the Frenchman's post. A table was laid in the middle of the room, overflowing with desserts . . .

"I am from Provence", the Frenchman explained. "And, where I come from, we prepare thirteen desserts for Christmas, in memory of Jesus and his twelve apostles."

The two men dug into the feast. They talked about their lives and their families and discovered they had the same hobbies . . . It was an excellent dinner, spiced up with laughter and funny stories!

When it was over, the German customs officer rose to leave with regret. "Merry Christmas!" he said. The two friends shook hands, and the German went back to his side of the border. As he said good-bye, he waved the white napkin the Frenchman had given him. By the light of the lantern, it looked like

the flag of peace.

The Christmas Eve Visitors

Old Jeremy was in such a state. Last night in a dream, Jesus had told him that he would come visit him this evening. But this evening was Christmas Eve. Jeremy had spent all day preparing the house. He had vacuumed, decorated the living room, set a beautiful table, and cooked a turkey with chestnuts. Jeremy was straightening his best bow tie when the front doorbell rang.

66

"Already!" he exclaimed. "He's early!"

Jeremy ran to open the door. What a disappointment! It was not Jesus at the door; just his neighbor, Miss Little.

"I'm sorry to disturb you, Mr. Jeremy, but I've run out of eggs for my omelet. Could I borrow one from you?"

"Yes, yes", answered Jeremy a little impatiently.

The old gentleman ran to the kitchen and came back with an egg in his hand.

"It's so sad to spend Christmas Eve all alone, don't you think?" continued his neighbor, who would really have liked to chat a moment.

"True, true", Jeremy grumbled. "Goodbye, Miss Little", he added, as he showed her gently out the door. "And Merry Christmas!" As Jeremy went back to light the candles on the table, someone knocked on the door.

"I'm coming!" he said with glee.

Another disappointment! It was only a beggar who had come to ask for a few coins for Christmas.

"That turkey with chestnuts smells good", the poor man remarked, his eyes gleaming with hunger. "I haven't eaten that in such a long time."

"Yes, yes, off you go! Take this", answered Jeremy, as he handed him a dollar bill. "And Merry Christmas!" he added, pushing him gently to the exit.

Jeremy closed the door and looked at his watch: eight thirty.

"Jesus won't be long now", he thought. And, indeed, a light tap on the door made him jump. But it was still not Jesus! It was Paul, the little boy from upstairs.

"What do you want?" Jeremy asked him a little sternly.

"Mommy had to do the night shift", the little boy answered. "She left me all alone because no one could babysit on Christmas Eve. I'm scared!"

"Come, come, be brave!" Jeremy said to him.

The little boy looked with envy at the brightly lit apartment. He would have liked to stay and sleep there.

"Here, this is for you", said Jeremy, handing him some candies. "Go back to bed now", he added, leading him back to the stairway. And then Jeremy waited, and waited, and waited . . . Eventually, the turkey got cold, the candles melted, and Jeremy dozed off. Jesus appeared to him once again in his sleep.

"Lord, you didn't come", Jeremy reproached him.

"Yes, I did!" Jesus answered. "I came three times, but you never invited me to stay!"

Jeremy woke with a start. He looked at his watch: it was not that late! He quickly hurried off to find Miss Little, the beggar, and Paul. And this time, he invited all three of them, and together they spent the most beautiful Christmas Eve ever.

The Angels' Christmas

"Sorry . . . excuse me! I'd just like to get past . . ."

Angelico, the littlest cherub in heaven, is trying to make his way through the middle of the crowd of angels. Today is a great day. Just imagine: the Son of the good Lord is to be born on earth; a baby, just like any other! Angelico would not miss this for anything in the world.

Honestly, the boss always has such wonderful ideas. If men do not understand that he loves them more than anything after this . . . !

In the meantime, Angelico is very annoyed. He was hoping to weave his way unnoticed up to the big balcony of paradise, the place closest to men. That way, he would have a front-row seat. But he was not the only angel who had the same idea!

And now, here are the angel musicians rehearsing the Gloria at full blast! The trumpet is very nice, but not right in your face, thank you very much! "You could try not to blow right in my ear!" Angelico complains.

"Sorry, little fellow, but everything's got to be ready to welcome the Son of the Almighty", retorts a handsome angel musician. And he blows his instrument even harder.

Ouch! An angel passing by has just whacked him on the head with his wing. The cherub is dazed. So he sits down on a fluffy little cloud, nice and comfy, until he can get his wits back. And then a great silence falls. "Oh no!" Angelico says to himself, "I lost track of the time! I must have missed it; the holy child is born!" But there is no Gloria. There must be some mistake. Angelico calls to an angel passing by his cloud.

"Excuse me, could you tell me what's happening?"

"Shush! It's the archangels. They've come to take their place on the Grand Balcony."

The archangels! Angelico has never seen them before, but he has heard so much about them.

Most of all, he has
heard about Gabriel, who had
the honor of asking Mary to become
the mother of little Jesus. Here they come,
passing before him.

How big they are, how beautiful! But, . . .
oh, careful! Gabriel is about to trip over a little cloud
and tumble into the heavenly orchestra! Angelico
blows on the cloud with all his might. Phew, just
in time. Gabriel hardly feels the cloud slip
beneath his wing. He turns to Angelico and
says, "Thank you, little angel. But you're
too little; you won't see anything from here.
Come with us to the Grand Balcony!"

Angelico cannot believe his ears. Here
he is on Gabriel's shoulders in the best possible
spot to watch the greatest event an angel could
ever see. He leans forward and holds his breath.
In the heavens, the angels fall silent.

Shh! The most beautiful night in the history
of the world is about to begin . . .

The Announcement to Herod

King Herod is in a nasty mood. He has slept very badly and has not been able to take his nap. From under a silk cushion, he grumbles, "What kind of a palace is this, with everyone breezing in and out whenever he feels like it!"

Knock, knock, knock! Herod gives a start. "Grrrr!" yells Herod. "What idiot has come to disturb me this time!"

A servant enters sheepishly on tiptoe.

He bows down before Herod. "Master, I, I . . . I'm sorry to disturb you. Three men are asking to see you. They've come from far away; they look very rich."

Very rich? Herod's temper cools down at once.

"Do you know what they want?" he asks.

"Good master, I can't make any sense of it: they're talking about a star, about gifts to be given to a king . . . About gold, about . . ."

"Quick, have them come in!" Herod interrupts him, rubbing his hands. "And just how many kings do you know of here? The gifts are for me!"

The servant hurries out. Herod runs quickly to sit on his throne and put on his crown, just in case the visitors do not immediately realize that he is the king. You never know with foreigners . . .

The door opens, and the servant makes way to let in three handsome gentlemen dressed in costly fabrics. They kneel down before Herod, who looks greedily at the three chests they place at his feet.

"What can I do for you, dear friends?" asks Herod in honeyed tones.

"We are three wise men in search of a king who has been born", says the first.

"We have traveled a long way to bring him these gifts of gold, incense, and myrrh», adds the second.

"We have seen his star shining. Can you tell us where the birth took place?" asks the third.

Another king besides him! So important that a star heralds his birth! Herod's anger boils again.

But he is sly and manages to stay calm. "A little king, how wonderful", he says in a gentle voice. "No, I have no idea where he was born . . . But, I'll go ask all the scholars in my palace. When you find this newborn king, please come and let me know. I, too, would like to go bow down before him."

"Agreed", say the three men as they take their leave.

As soon as they are out of the door, Herod explodes with rage. He throws his crown on the floor and yells at the poor servant, «I want this new king found and destroyed!»

Meanwhile, the three wise men go to Bethlehem and adore the newborn Christ Child, giving him their gifts. Afterward, warned in a dream not to return to Herod, they go back home by another route.

The Nativity

What a multitude of people in Bethlehem! Joseph and his wife, Mary, who is pregnant, try to weave their way through the crowds. It has already been several days since they set out from their home in Nazareth, in Galilee, to come to the town of Bethlehem, in Judea. They have come to be enrolled in the census in the city of the family of Joseph, because Emperor Augustus has ordered the counting of all the inhabitants of the empire.

Exhausted from the journey, Mary is riding on a donkey. The time for the birth of her baby has almost arrived. Joseph has knocked on every door, trying to find somewhere to stay.

His face is grave and worried. "Our baby can't be born in the street … But, there's no place for us anywhere in Bethlehem, even at the inn …"

Night is falling. Joseph pushes open a stable door. Mary gets down off the donkey and smiles. "We'll be fine here, Joseph, far from the noise of the crowd. The ox and the donkey surely won't mind making a little room for us!" Joseph and Mary unload their bags and settle into the fresh hay.

It is almost midnight. Mary's baby is born. She wraps him in swaddling clothes and lays him in the hay in the animals' manger. Joseph does not know what to do or say. He grips his walking-stick and prays for the infant and his mother. He sings praises to God for this baby whom God has entrusted to him and promises to look after him always.

Not far from there, outside Bethlehem, shepherds are in the fields, watching over their flocks through the night. Suddenly, an angel appears to them, saying, "Do not be afraid! I come to announce to you the good news of great joy for all people! This night a Savior has been born for you.

"He is the Messiah, the Lord. He comes to bring you light, peace, and joy. You will find him wrapped in swaddling clothes and lying in a manger." All of a sudden, thousands of angels appear in the sky, praising God and singing, "Glory to God in the highest, and peace on earth to those he loves."

"Let's go to Bethlehem!" the shepherds say to one another. "Quick! Let's hurry to go find this good news from God." They set off with their flocks. When they arrive at the stable, they find Mary, Joseph, and the newborn lying in a manger, just as the angel told them. They do not dare say a word. They fall to their knees in wonder, praising God for this child who has come to bring them light and joy. All is calm in the stable.

Mary contemplates her child and adores him. She does not understand it all, but she keeps everything that has happened in her heart. Joseph has fallen asleep, exhausted, leaning on his cane. The ox and the gray donkey keep watch through the night, breathing on the baby to keep him nice and warm.